Made in United States
Orlando, FL
28 May 2023

33515770R00074